KB037477

책방에서 빗소리를 들었다

김은지 지음

이수경 옮김

디자인이음

차례

Contents

Part 3

1부

솔잎

노란 바늘잎이
무릎에 떨어졌다

언젠가 당신 만나게 되면
솔잎이 언제 떨어지는지 아느냐고 물어보리라
다른 사람에게는 물어보지 않고
솔잎에 대해 궁금해하면서 살아가리라

뭉게구름이 조금 움직였고
운동장 트랙과 그늘이 선명해졌고
개미가 지나가고 있었다

책방에서 빗소리를 들었다

내 마음은
비 오는 날을 위해
만들어졌다

난 내일 필 거야
그건 벚꽃의 계획

그러나 가지마다
다랑다랑
빗방울 꽃 피는 것을

몰랐다
이렇게 예쁜데
왜 비 오는 날마다
보러 나오지 않은 거지

나는 너무 내 마음을 몰랐다

비가 와서 산에 안 가고
서점엘 갔다
그래서 비가 온 것이
그렇게 좋았다

지붕을 내려다본다
지붕은
비 오는 날을 위해
뾰족한 모양을 하고 있다

내 마음은
비 오는 날을 위해
만들어졌다

마리아나 해구*

해적의 노래를 부르며 간다
그동안 얼마를 모았건
얼마를 잃었건
아이야 아오아
양팔에 힘을 주고 타륜을 돌리자

돛이 그리는 구름이
물살을 따라 뛰노는 물고기가
모두 내 것이라고 해도
그저 아오아 아이야
속도를 높일 뿐

맥주를 부어라
넌 어디서 왔다고 했지?
네가 저지른 바보 같은 짓이 뭐라고?

아이야 아오아

아오아 아이야

어서 부어라

네가 못 이룬 꿈이

너를 찼다는 그이가

맥주의 맛을 좋게 하는구나

달을 던지면서

별을 박으면서

아이아오아

고래가 뛰어오른다

* 가장 깊은 바다

마취

물고기 떼가 지나간다
왜냐하면 여기는 그들의 영역이니까
레몬 레몬
아쿠아블루
이 물고기들은 어째서
이렇게 화려한 색을 가질 수 있지

물고기 떼를 따라간다
나는 민트
먼 미래에 나는 민트색 스트라이프를 가지게 될
것이다
왜냐하면 갖고 싶은 것을 골랐기 때문에

나는 예전에 물 밖으로 나오면서
기쁨을 분비하는 꼬리지느러미를 두고 왔다

*

이제 곧 새가 지저귈 것이다

솔 레 파

솔 레 파샵

위로만 올리는 음계는 발끝을 오므리게 한다

태양을 끌어당기느라

안 꺼냈던 태양을 꺼내느라

다른 둥지를 재촉하느라

이윽고 동이 트고

나무마다 잎파랑이*가 켜진다

—

나는 시계도 없이 네 시 오십 분이면 지저귄다

701동 여자는 오늘도

*엽록소

15

이마 이마
미간 미간
콧잔등 콧잔등하며
잠이 들려고 애쓰고 있다

하기 싫은 머리를 하고
가기 싫은 나라를 가 본다
숨어 있는 세계를 끌어당기듯

이윽고 동이 트고
잠이 켜진다

*

때가 되면 기울어지는 시간
도마뱀처럼 손을 편다
어제까지 연두색이었으면서

조금 전까지도 연두색이었으면서

아무도 없을 때는 괜찮았어?

그럼 어렸을 때는?

십 년 전에는?

십 년 후에는?

나는 도마뱀처럼 손을 펴고 붙어 있다

조금 전까지도 연두색이었으면서

금방 사과색이 된다

힘을 빼고 싶어

떨어지게 두고 싶어

튜닝 페그*

밤마다 새집을 짓고
아침이면 집을 거두는
거미가 있어

사람들은 거미에 대한 이야기도 하고
미국 대통령 후보가 했다는 믿을 수 없는 말을
주고받았다

나는 나무 계단에 앉아서
우쿨렐레를 튜닝했다

네, 남편은 잘 지내고 있어요
오늘 출장이라서 올 수 없었어요

나는 페이스북에서
그 남자가 이혼을 했고

새로운 시작을 위해 일본으로 떠났다는 포스팅을
봤지만

튜닝기를 켜고도
어떤 높이의 C 코드가 기준이 되는지
알 수 없었다

내가 앉았던 나무 계단에는 다음 날
뱀이 지나갔다
독이 없는 착한 뱀이라고 했다

거미의 집을 보려고
새벽에 일어났다

* Tuning peg : 우쿨렐레의 줄감개

염소의 예방 접종

동그라미나 네모로 자르고 싶다

나를 기억하기 위한 색은 두 가지만
단 두 가지 색으로 팬더와 같은 특별함을
다른 이별과 겹치지 않게

간단한 레고 블록에 상상력이 더 발휘되듯이
가뜬한 추억에서 더 생생함을 느낄 수 있도록

어차피 잊혀질 이름이며 목소리
표정
뒷모습

미워하는 일은 너무 복잡해
한철 어려워한 다음, 곧 잊어버리게 될 것이다

당신을 떠올리는 날을 두 가지만
다른 이별과 겹치지 않게

낮달이 뜬 날과
양지에서도 얼어 있던 눈
이제 녹는 날

먼저 낮달이 뜬 하늘을
세모꼴로 오리자

혼자 여행하기의 어려움

할아버지 벽시계에 밥 먹이던 열쇠를 생각할 때와

손이 못생긴 걸 들킬까 봐 숨길 때
손 못생긴 거 상관없이 편해질 때도

쓰지 않는 재봉틀을 밟아
페달의 공회전 소리를 듣고 있을 때

누군가가 막 너무

자동판매기 조명이 쨍한 여름밤
비디오를 빌려보기로 하고 나설 때와 비슷하다

종이가방이 터져 떨어진 물건을 거둘 때도

한강과 여의도를 바라보다가
호퍼라면 강변북로를 보겠구나 싶은 순간에도

다리의 다리를 보고 있을 때의 그런

오소리가 나타난다는 내리막
내리막을 뛰어내려와 봤던 옥수숫대의 싱그러움
그 뽀드득한 껍데기에 손을 대어 볼 때처럼

곶감 말리는 창고 속을 채운 빛 먼지와
혹은 언덕길을 오를 때 우산 속에서 켜지는 자의식
처럼

쓰지 않는 재봉틀을 밟아
페달의 공회전 소리를 듣고 있을 때

옆 사람의 신발 끈이 풀린 것을 봤을 때도

누군가를 막 너무

왼쪽 페달

이 섬에서 나는 사슴을 기다렸다

불가사리를 구경하다가
굴 한 바구니를 담아 오기도 하고
딱따구리가 보였다가 안 보였다가 하는 나무 아래서
낮잠을 자기도 했다

금빛 풀숲에서
풀보다 키 작은 토끼를 쫓아다니고
옛날 종이를 만들었다는 공장의 차가운 물레를
양팔로 안아 보았다

그런 걸 말해 줘서 고마워

굴 껍데기 위에 촛불을 켜고
물개와 고래에 대해 적혀 있는 나무 기둥에 기대어

고래 떼가 지나가는 길을 그려 보면서
나는 내내 사슴이 나타나기를 기다렸다

　네 마음만 생각해
　다른 사람은 생각하지 마

고루 뻗은 뿔
물을 뜨러 가던 나를 응시하는 새까만 눈을
사라지는 다음 장면은 없는
말처럼 커다란 몸을

촛농이 다 녹을 때까지 나는 아무 말도 하지 않았고
이 섬에서는 아무도
나를 본 일이 없다고 했다

대여

모르는 사람의 집에 머무르고 있다
발코니에 나와
길 건너 있는 정원의 분수를 보고 있다

모르는 사람은 아마 여자인 것 같다
욕실에 여러 종류의 바디워시가 있다

침대 속으로 들어갈 때
이불을 들다 멈칫했다
괜찮을까요,

사자와 포도와 아이들이 나오는 꿈속에서
물을 마시고
심각한 고민을 하고
높은 곳에서 떨어졌다

발코니에 나와 분수를 본다

장미 냄새가 난다

따뜻하게 달아오른 철제 의자에

등을 기댄다

지진

　게이오 대학 근처의 한 사무실에서 호스피스 회원
들과 인터뷰를 하던 도중 잠시 화장실에 갔다
　손에 비누칠을 하는 사이 꽤 큰 지진이 일었다
　회색 벽이 들썩였다
　사무실로 돌아왔을 때
　인터뷰를 기다리던 네 명의 노인 모두
　내가 크게 놀랐을까 걱정했다며
　담담한 나를 보고 안심했다
　나를 바라보는 그들 모두 웃는 얼굴이었지만
　양팔을 축 늘어뜨린 채 앉아 있었다

2부

붓

눈을 떴을 때
언니와 오빠가 나를 내려다보고 있었다

어서 일어나라고,
삼촌이 죽었다고 했다

나는 죽었다는 말이 무슨 뜻인지 몰랐기 때문에
구석으로 밀려 있는 소파에 가서
더 자도 되느냐고 물었다

명절처럼 사람들이 집으로 왔고
나는 사촌 언니가 온 것이 좋았다

고모들은 계속 울다가
손님들이 올 때마다 다시 울었다

고모 좀 봐 울지 말라고 하면서 자기가 울어
진짜네 웃기다

굿판이 끝나고 엄마는
나의 머리카락을 쓸어 주며 말했다
삼촌은 아마 참새가 되었을 거야
너무 착한 사람이니까

그러자 눈물이 나기 시작했다

눈을 떴을 때
비디오 액정의 네온 파랑이
언제나 맞지 않는 시간으로 깜빡이고 있었다

화첩의 첫 번째 그림
-옥순봉도*

사공은 노를 저어 간다
갓을 쓴 이 둘 태우고

멀리 가리키고 있는 이의
느리고 능청스런 말투
들릴 듯한데

엄마가 수영하며 자란 강

외삼촌이 발을 헛디뎠다는 다리도
여기 어디려나

나는 상선암 강가에서 멀미를 하고
아빠는 중선암 근처에 차를 세워 담배를 태웠다

발밑에 솟는 물줄기

바위를 넘나들고

여기 한 발자국만 내디디면 죽겠구나
쑤욱 빨려들겠구나 싶은데도 난
푸르른 물살 가까이 다가갔다

미술관 진열대에 얼굴을 바짝 대고
갓을 쓴 사람들을 본다

비 온 뒤 죽순 같다고
옥순봉이라 해요

*단원 화첩의 첫 번째 그림

마지막 문장

엄마가 당신이 쓴 시를 읽어 보라고 줬다

나는 다 좋은데 마지막 문장이 좀 뜬금없다고 했다
엄마는 니가 뭘 아냐며, 내가 지금까지 살아오면서
신문에서 읽어온 시가 얼마며,
문창과에 다닌다는 애가 이제 보니 시에 대해 아무
것도 모르네, 라며
엉크렇게 화를 냈다

그게 아니라 나는 일이삼사 연이 다 좋다, 다 좋은데
이건 이래서 좋고 저건 저래서 좋고
마치 내가 금강산을 다녀온 느낌까지 들었다
이런 표현은 어떻게 떠오른 거냐, 찬찬히 내 감상을
전한 뒤
그런데 마지막에 이런 마무리는 일기 같다 랄까 아쉽
다고 했다

엄마는 그러니까 니가 시를 뭘 아냐며, 내가 지금
까지 신문에서 읽어온 시가 얼마며

봄가을이면 백일장에서 매번 상금도 타 오고

누구 엄마도 읽어 보더니 도대체 어떻게 이렇게 글
을 잘 쓰냐며 그랬는데 넌 뭐냐 라며 화를 냈다

엄마가 이렇게 화를 내는 사람이었다니

내가 뭐 시를 못 썼다고 한 것도 아니고

한 문장 정도 이견을 가질 수 있는 것 아니냐

문장을 지적하는 게 이렇게 기분 나쁜 거였나 문창
과 친구들은 정말 강철 심장을 가졌구나, 하는 생각
이 들었다

저녁을 차릴 때엔 한발 물러나

엄마, 아마 내가 시를 많이 못 읽어 봐서 이런 표현
방식에 익숙하지 못한가 봐요,

37

어렵게 말을 건네 봤다

그러자 그건 정말이지 니가 몰라서 이해를 못하는 거다 라며

그 마지막 문장은 아무런 문제가 없다고 했다

엄마가 이렇게 오래 화를 안 푸는 사람이었다니

나는 처음으로 엄마가 아니라 허만분 씨를 화나게 만들었다

엄마 다시 보니 마지막 문장이 괜찮아요

어제는 미안해요

다음 날 사과까지 했지만

사과는 전혀 통하지 않았다

엄마는 계속 시를 쓰고 있다

엄마가 엄마 얘기 글로 쓰지 말라고 몇 번이나 말 했는데

자꾸 엄마 얘기를 쓰게 된다

생각해 보면 엄마의 마지막 문장은 그렇게 일기 같지도 않았다

눈썹, 셔터 우선*

어느 방향으로 무릎을 꿇는 것인지 몰라서
왠지 창이 난 쪽으로 할게요

자판기 조명을 등지고
기도합니다

제발 잠을 주소서
부디 오늘밤 엄마에게
잠을 하나 내려 주소서

우리에게 매일 밤 내려 주시는
치료의 잠을 주소서
망각의 잠을 주소서

고라니에게도 사자에게도 의사에게도
밤이면 하나씩 자비롭게

나눠 주시는

휴게실에서 나와 간호사와 마주쳤을 때
나를 가엽게 보는 처진 눈썹

그 외에 모두
흐려진다

*움직이는 사물을 찍을 때 사용하는 기능

불 냄새

모래톱엔 아무도 없었고
읍내로 들어가는 버스를 기다리느라
정류소에서 한 시간을 떨었다

모닥불 태운 자리엔
빈 막걸리 병

내가 아는 누군가
넋 놓고 앉았을 걸 생각하니

불 너머
열기에 흔들리는
허한 표정을 본 마냥
눈가가 따가워졌다

일인식 식당

여자는 일본 가정식을 먹고
나는 여자의 먹는 소리를 듣는다

여자는 친절한 사람일까?
이 늦은 밤에 무슨 일이 있었을까?

여자는 표현이 서툰 사람이다
최근에 힘든 일을 잘 이겨냈다

아니 여자는 어떻지도 않고
나는 여자에 대해 그 어떤 생각도 하지 않는다

수사자처럼
초목과 코끼리와 습도에 감응하는 모든 방식을
바꿔가고 있다
귓불을 누르며

삭제!

그릇에 오늘치의 온기가 나왔다
옆에 앉은 사람은
온기를 빨리 먹고 나갔다

국그릇에 연보라색 꽃이 그려져 있고
나는 그 꽃의 이름을 모른다
꽃이 무엇인지 찾아보지 않을 것이다

누군가 앉았을 때
내가 있는 그대로 대한 사람이
한 명 늘어났다

메세나폴리스로 간다

저 야식집에
나는 앉혀 있었다

말을 고르는 그의 뒤로
벌레 한 마리가 벽을 오르고 있었다

뒤에,

라고 말했고
둘이서 벌레가 올라가는 것을 바라보았다

상기된 얼굴로 말을 고르는 그에게 내가 무슨 말을
했는지
아무리 기억해 보려고 해도 기억나지 않는다

망설이다가

뒤에, 라고 말한 것만 생각이 난다

벌레를 잡기도 그렇고
그냥 보고 있었던 것만 기억이 난다

십 년 전 내가 살았던 집은
옷 가게와 부동산이 되어 있고

합정역 5번 출구 앞 사진관에는
같은 가족사진이 걸려 있다

서보 기구

보습 학원에서 수업을 하고
중간에 김밥과 튀김우동을 먹는다

모르는 단어들을 발음하며
샛길에 있는 메타세콰이어의 무른 수피를
꾹꾹 누른다

조타 장치 :
사람 대신에 정해진 침로를 유지하는 '서보 기구'

서보 기구 :
장치의 입력이 임의로 변할 때 출력을 설정한 목푯
값에 이르도록 제어하는 장치

조타 장치 :
나를 집으로 돌아오게 하는 내 신발들의 기억력

서보 기구 :

밤 11시 유재석이 나오는 예능 프로그램

내가 했던 크고 작은 행동들이 떠오른다

의외의 순서로

반대의 온도로

모르는 단어들을 발음하며

샛길에 있는 메타세콰이어의 무른 수피를

꾹꾹 누른다

기쁨을 후회하면서

후회를 기뻐하면서

내가 아는 어떤 사람이

내가 아는 어떤 사람이 이혼하고 나서 아이를 갖고
싶어졌다 나는 자전거를 타고 가다가 그를 생각했다
내가 아는 어떤 사람이 택시 타고 가라고 오천 원을
쥐여 주었다 나는 자전거를 타고 가다가 그를 생각했
다 내가 아는 어떤 사람이 결국 보험에 가입하지 못
했다 물냉면이 맵다고 눈물 흘리고 코를 풀었다

내가 아는 어떤 사람이 일을 구하지 못하고 고국으
로 돌아갔다 아내와 아들은 여기 머무르고 있다 나는
자전거를 타고 가다가 그를 생각했다 내가 아는 어떤
사람이 연락처에서 나를 지웠다 나는 자전거를 타고
가다가 그를 생각했다

내가 아는 어떤 사람이 애매한 순간에 길을 건넜다
나는 자전거를 타고 가다가 그를 생각했다 내가 아는
어떤 사람이 며느리 몰래 한글을 배웠다 나는 자전거
를 타고 가다가 그를 생각했다 내가 아는 어떤 사람

이 건조한 방에 허브를 사다 놓았다 얼마 뒤에는 선인장을 사다 놓았다 나는 자전거를 타고 가다가 그를 생각했다

　내가 아는 사람의 아는 사람의 아는 사람의 아는 사람이 자기한테 투자를 하라고 했다 나는 자전거를 타고 가다가 그를 생각했다 내가 아는 어떤 사람이 연락처에서 나를 지웠다 나는 자전거를 타고 가다가 모르는 사람을 생각했다 내가 모르는 어떤 사람이 목련과 동백을 반대로 말했다 나는 목련과 동백을 생각했다

망고

학원은 다음 달 폐업을 결정했다
오 학년 승원이를 못 본다면 서운할 것이다
승원이가 공부하는 미국독립혁명은 1775년부터
1783년까지다
토머스 제퍼슨 옆에 앉은 프랭클린이 피뢰침을 만든
그 프랭클린일 줄은
승원이는 머리카락을 뽑는다
정수리에 피가 난 것을 본 것은 지난 가을이었는데
지금은 동전 크기만큼 두피가 보인다

오월이다
수학여행 소풍 죄다 취소되어 애들이 학원으로
온다
지금쯤이면 제주도 공항에 도착했을 텐데
아냐 이미 도착했지 바보야 일출봉 갔겠지
이런 걸로 언성을 높이며 오 분만 놀게 해 달라고
오 분 동안 재잘거린다

놀게 해 줬더니 놀지는 않고

사망자와 실종자와 구조자의 수를 외운다며 말을
시킨다

꿈에서 삼 층만한 파도를 봤단다

화장실 문에 끼는 꿈을 꿨단다

올 들어 망고가 자주 보인다

크기가 작아서 산 적은 없었는데 트럭에 놓인 망고
가 꽤 크다

조금만 더 자란다면 저 보드라운 껍질 속에 싱그러
운 여름을 담겠지

조금만 더 기다리면

망고라니

가슴이 아파서 망고는 먹을 수가 없다

가까운 사이

그녀에게 전화를 건다
그녀는 우유를 사러 가는 길이라고 한다
소문에 대해서는 말을 하지 않는다
언제 그토록 많은 일이 있었던 거지?
우리의 지난 시간은 그녀에 대해서 아무것도 설명
해 주지 못한다

그녀는 새벽 공기를 마시고 감기에 걸린 적도 없고
맥주 캔을 찌그리기에 적당한 둔치도
마땅히 울 만한 낡은 벽돌 성당의 벤치도
알지 못한다

다시 태어나야 해?

하긴
다시 태어나면 무엇이 되고 싶냐고 내가 물었을 때

그녀는 오히려 되물었던 것이다

다행이라고
목소리를 확인할 수 있어서

비가 오려는 지금 낙엽
밟는 소리가 포근하다

묘연

만화책을 선물 받았다
그것은 만화책 쪽보다는 선물 쪽에 가까운 것이었다
하지만 그것은 너무 재미있어서
언니 친구가 빌려 갔다

선물 받은 거니까 꼭 돌려 달라고 했는데
결국 돌려받지 못했고
언니는 누가 빌려 갔는지 알려 주지도 않고
곤란한 표정을 지을 뿐이었다

만화책이 다시 보고 싶어서
사촌 언니에게 빌렸다
　소장하고 싶은 거니까 꼭 돌려줘
사촌 언니는 강조하며 빌려줬다

아주 재미있게 읽고

이번에 만날 땐 돌려줘야지 생각했지만
한 번 더 읽고 싶은 마음에 미루고 있다

그래도 이것은 선물이 아니다
내가 받은 선물은 아니다

이른 새벽 택시 안에서
만화책의 행방을 떠올린다
왜 잃어 버렸는지 알면서도

3부

퇴직 축하 모임

오셔서 함께 해 주세요
당신을 초대합니다

나의 생일,
내가 결정한

이제 다른 삶을 살아가기로 결정했어요

나를 위해 술을 한잔 올리고
춤을 출 거예요

계약서 싸인 야근수당 택시비 나이 통신비 성장률
그리고 부모님
그리고 사람들 이야기 이야기

아아, 너무나 불안하고

죄책감이 몰려오지만

그것이 확 설렘으로 변하는
그것을 문득 기대로 바꾸는
파티를 열어요

당신의 응원과 함께라면
난 기대가 됩니다

아니 그냥 다 잊고
우리 그냥 만나요
퇴직은 핑계

노을공원 캠핑장에서 새우 요리 해 먹으면서
좋아하는 사람들
얼굴 보아요

오후의 벚꽃

벚꽃이 뛰어내린다

이번에 불어오는 바람을 타자
난 저 작은 회오리를 탈 거야

소르르
바람을 일으키는 나비의 날개와
높이높이 오르는 꽃잎

문 앞에 내려앉은 꽃잎은
어디 멀리 다니고 온 것일까

이제 곧
기다리던 손님이 도착할 시간

벚나무 내려다보며

나무들의

파도 소리를 듣는다

철길

설악초 잎은
흰색 바탕에
초록이 조금만 있어서
잎이 꽃 같고 꽃이 잎 같아

이젠 기차가 다니지 않는 철길

카페 주인은
장터에
헌 물건 구경하러 나왔다

잎이 꽃 같고
꽃이 잎 같아

잎은 꽃 같지만
꽃은 꽃 같은데?

교복 바지를 입은 여학생들이 철길 위를 걷고
소리 지르던 아저씨는 강아지와 산책을 하고
헌 물건은 새 주인을 찾았다

새하얀 아스팔트
파도치는 건널목
오후만큼 아무렇지 않은 나
이런 것들을 상상하고 있으면

은행나무 잎이
하늘색으로 물든다

축제

술을 마시고 손을 맞잡고
가장 슬픈 이야기를 하나씩 털어놓았다

형이 잘못 사는 얘기
그녀가 잘못 떠난 얘기
질투, 못지않은 억울함
정체를 알 수 없는 가난

손 잡은 사람 이야기에 울고 있는데
화장실에 갔던 한 명이 뛰어나와
이거 십오 일 전에 삼켰던 약이 명치에 걸려 있었
나 봐 라며
토해 낸 알약을 보여 줬다

우리는 모두 기뻐 일어나
술상을 가운데에 두고 박수를 치며 춤을 추려는데

창가에서, 벽을 사이에 두고 있다는 것을 믿을 수
없게 가까운 소리로
"이제 그만 잡시다. 좀."
옆집 사람의 한 마디

잠에서 깼을 때
우리가 꺼낸 알약은 보이지 않았다
꾸벅 꾸벅
약이 놓여 있었던 것 같은 곳을
쓸어 보았다

단 한 사람

말차 케이크 속에
산딸기 잼이 들어 있다

나라면
말차만으로 만들었을 텐데

언니, 산딸기 맛이 없었더라면
심심했을 거예요

그런가
그래서 내가 안되나 봐

뭐가요?

응?
(가장 잘 쓰는
단 한 사람)

조금 더
조금 더 힘내서 되어 보고 싶다
가장 잘 쓰는 단 한 사람
나에게는 산딸기 잼이 필요하다!

산딸기 잼이라…

사발을 들고 꿀꺽꿀꺽 마시던 말차의 맛
그리고 내쉬던
초록 입김

역시 난
말차만으로.

단 한 사람이 되는 건?

못하겠어요

정해진 빛을 보는 방식

당신이 꾸는 꿈을 상상해요
아주 깊은 밤에
분홍색 담배를 물고
담배의 맛은
여름

솔직히 내 꿈에선
별다른 일이 일어나지 않아요
여기저기 가고
억울하면 울곤 하지요
왜인지
공간은 한껏 구체적이지만

당신이 꾸는 꿈을 상상해요
직접 그리고 싶어
크레용을 뺏으려는 아이처럼

아니,
새를 그려 달라고
드로잉북을 내미는 기분으로

사랑한다는 걸 증명하려면
사랑하지 않는다는 걸 말해야 하고
사랑하지 않는다는 걸 증명하려면
사랑한다고 말해야 하는 꿈
(그런데 누구에게 증명하는 건지)

벽에 등을 꼭 붙이고
나에게 들킬까 봐 늘
숨어 다니는 마음

꿈을 꿔요
꿈을 잘 꿀 것 같은 사람의 것으로

술병에 그려진 흰곰,

단팥빵을 빠르게 포장하는 기술,

나를 진정시키는 모르는 단어,

어제 발표된 시

그럼 당신은

원하는 꿈을 꿀 수 있나요?

보고 싶은 사람을

꿈에 나타나게 할 수 있나요?

진짜로 생각을 많이 하면 (웃음)

자기 전에 계속 생각하면 (웃음)

너무나 무능한 난

엊그제 꾼 꿈에 사로잡혀 있어요

멀리까지 내다볼 수 있는 언덕 위의 집이 보이고요
일 층의 작은 식당이에요
가까운 사람들과 함께 있었지만
난 누군가를 기다리게 만들어서
조바심이 났답니다

확인할 순 없지만
거의 확실해요
나는 다른 사람 꿈에 나타납니다

누구도 등장인물을 고를 수 없으니까
누가 나타나면
내쫓을 순 없으니까

확인할 순 없지만
거의 확실해요

내가 기다리게 했지요

그 꿈에서

부탁했지요

나를 진정시키는 모르는 단어,

어제 발표된 시

난

정해진 대로

빛을 보고 싶진 않아요

'있어 주기'

'잊어 주기'

부탁한 것의 굴절

꿈을 꾸어요

꿈을 잘 꿀 것 같은 사람의 것으로

마음이 다가와
옆에 앉듯이

막

나는 두 시에 몰두한다

두 시는 노른자가 납작한 계란프라이

너 그렇게 그렇지 않아

네가 정색할 때 내려앉은 가슴

나는 두 시에 몰두한다

두 시는 내내 자고 일어났지만 여전히 할 일 없는

강아지의 문제

기억나지 않는 축구 경기

기억나지 않는 내가 했다던 말

네 말을 듣고 서 있던 내 발꿈치

나는 세 시 십구 분에 몰두한다

누우면 가로세로가 바뀌듯

누워도 가로세로가 바뀌지 않듯

하얀 보자기 끝자락 주름을 펴며

네가 내 이름을 불러주기 전부터

나는 나였고
네가 즈려 밟고 간 뒤에도 꽃은 꽃

꽃이 쏟아지는 세 시 십구 분에 나는 몰두한다
활주로로 향하는 엔진 소리
지금 내가 사는 동네를 결정한 우연
우연보다 앞선 우연
밤의 세 시 십구 분은 뭉쳐 있고
흔들리고 흩어지는 새벽의 세 시 십구 분은

내가 남긴 국수를 먹는 남자의 표정
그날 입었던 옷
쭉 당겼다가 탁 쏘아지는 활처럼
네 시가 날아와 꽂힌다
네 시가 나에게 몰두한다
절연한 슬픔

절연하지 못하는 슬픔

그리워하던 나를 그리워하는 막막함

코끼리 같은 동물의 엉덩이를 중심으로 뒷모습

네 시도 나를 두고 간다

민트

심장이 커졌다
바위를 이식한 것 같아
운동화를 이식한 것 같아
토끼를 이식한 것 같아

꽃잎 한 장을 올려 주었지만
서쪽 창가에 널어 보았지만
왜일까
줄어들지 않는다

고양이가 숨는 덤불에
문틀을 만들고
재활용품을 내놓는 소리에
올리브유를 뿌린다
별에는 빨간 펜으로 오답 처리를 하고

꽉, 꽉, 꽉

트랙을 파낼 듯이 달린다
1.2배 속으로 재생되는 하루

그러니까 왜일까
커튼을 치고
현관문을 점검하고
심장을 가로로 뉘어 주었는데

아니어도 괜찮아
그리고 그건 좋은 거야
중요하지 않아
그리고 그건 좋은 거야

심장이 나를 데리고 간다
팍. 팍. 팍
더위를 버티지 못하게 한다
두 개의 삶을 일치시킨다

비디오테이프를 기리는 노래

비디오테이프라는 것이 있었다
그것은 가장 낭만적인 플라스틱

비디오 빌려 볼래, 라고 누가 말할 때
그건 영화 보러 갈래, 와는 다른 느낌

비디오를 보기로 해서
시험 끝난 날 나영이네 거실에 모였고
엄마가 서울 살던 수정이네 안방에 가 봤으니까

비디오가게의 필름 냄새는
말 내달리는 서부의 흙냄새
임청하가 손가락 끝으로 던진 물방울 냄새
중세 기사의 칼집 냄새

녹화 버튼을 누를 때 그 '따각'의 분명함이란

연체료를 깎아 줬을 때 홀가분함이란
앞으로 마구 착해지고 싶은 그 기분

결론은 이렇다*
비디오 가게가 하나씩 사라지면서
우리는 따로 떨어졌고
골목마다 비디오 가게가 있던 나날의 얼굴들은
여기 심장 가까이에 녹화되어 있다

* 파블로 네루다의 「내 양말을 기리는 노래」 마지막 연을 변주하였다.

I Heard the Sound of Raindrops at the Bookstore

Part 1

Pine Needles

A yellow pine needle

fell on my knee

If I meet you one day

I will ask when the pine needles fall

I won't ask anyone else

and live forever curious to know about the pine needles

Cumulus clouds moved slightly

The field track and shadows became clear

An ant was marching by

I Heard the Sound of Raindrops at the Bookstore

My mind
is made
for rainy days

I will bloom tomorrow
That is the cherry blossom's plan

I did not know
that raindrop flowers bloomed
on every branch

I did not know
So beautiful they were
Why did I not go see them
on every rainy day

I could not make up my mind enough

Because it rained

I went not to the mountain

but instead to the bookstore

I was so glad for rain to come

I look down at the roofs

The roofs

are sharp

for rainy days

My mind

is made

for rainy days

Mariana Trench*

I sail, singing a pirate song

No matter how much I gathered

or lost

Ah–ee–ya Ah–o–ah

Put strength in both arms and steer the wheel

Though the clouds

Drawn by the sails

And the fish that play in the current

are all mine

Ah–o–ah Ah–ee–ya

I only gather speed

Pour the beer

Where did you say you're from?

What foolish things have you done?

Aheeya Ahoah

Ahoah Aheeya

Hurry and pour

The dreams unmade

The one who left you

makes the beer taste good

Tossing the moon

Hammering the stars

Aheeahoah

A whale breaches

* The deepest part of the sea

Anesthesia

A school of fish pass by

This is their territory

Lemon lemon

Aqua blue

How do these fish

have such vibrant colors?

I follow a school of fish

For me, mint

In the far future, I will have mint stripes

Because I have chosen what I wanted

Long ago when I crawled out of the water

I left behind my caudal fin, that secreted happiness

*

Soon the birds will chirp

Sol, re, fa

Sol, re, F sharp

Scales that high make my toes curl

Pulling the sun,

Taking out the pristine sun,

Urging another nest,

Soon the dawn breaks

And the chlorophyll on each tree activates

—

Even without a watch I chirp at four fifty

The woman in the 701 complex

is trying so hard to fall asleep

Saying my forehead my forehead
my temples my temples
my nose my nose

Wearing a hairstyle she does not like
Visiting a country she does not like
As if she were pulling at a hidden world

Soon the dawn breaks
And sleep activates

*

Time tilts when ripe
I spread my hands like a lizard
Though I was yellow green just yesterday
Though I was yellow green just a little while ago,

Were you all right when there was nobody?

How about when you were young?

Ten years ago?

Ten years later?

I spread my hands and hang there like a lizard

Though I was yellow green just a little while ago,

I immediately turn into apple color

I want to relax my arms

And let myself fall

Tuning Peg*

There was a spider

which built a new web every night

and cleared it by daybreak

People talked about the spider

And also talked about things the American president

candidate said,

that were hard to believe

I sat on the wooden stairs

And tuned my ukulele

Yes, my husband is good

Today he's on a business trip and can't come

I saw

on Facebook

a post that he is divorced

and starting anew in Japan

I couldn't tell

which pitch of the C chord was the starting point

even with the tuner on

The next day a snake passed by

the wooden stair I had sat on

People told me that it was a nice snake with no

poison

I woke up at dawn

To see the spider's web

  * A ukulele's peg for strings

Goat Vaccination

I want to cut out a circle or a square

Two colors only to remember me
So that the two special colors, like the panda's,
do not overlap with other farewells

Just like the plain lego—blocks allow for more
imagination
So that the bland memories feel more vivid

Names, voices,
facial expressions
And the rear silhouettes will eventually be forgotten

Hating someone is too complicated
After a difficult period, it will be forgotten

Only remembering you on two kinds of days

So they do not overlap with other farewells

Days when the moon meets the sun

And days when the frozen snow in sunny spots

finally melts

For starters let's cut out a triangle

For the days when the moon meets the sun

The Difficulties of Traveling Alone

Whenever I think of the key that fed grandfather's wall clock

Whenever I hide my hands for fear of other people noticing their ugliness
And also the times I feel comfortable regardless

Whenever I push down on the unused sewing machine
And listen to the idling sound of the pedal

I wish someone would···

Similar to going out and borrowing videos
On summer nights when the vending machine lights are shining

Also, the times I must pick up the items from a torn paper bag

As I look at the Han River and Yeoui Island
I believe Hopper would look upon the Gangbyeon Expressway
Like looking at the legs of a bridge

Like the time I touched the smooth hard skin of fresh cornstalks
Fresh cornstalks I saw while running away, down the hill
The hill where the wild badger is said to live

Like the dust particles floating through the light of the persimmon shed
Like a sudden spur of self—consciousness

Whilst walking up a hill, under the cover of an umbrella

Whenever I push down on the unused sewing machine
And listen to the idling sound of the pedal

As well as the time when I saw the untied shoelaces of the person next to me

I need someone to⋯

Left Pedal

On this island I have been waiting for a deer

Watching starfish
I gathered a basket of oysters
Under the tree watching the woodpecker appear and
disappear
I napped

In the golden field of grass
I chased a rabbit smaller than the grass blades
I hugged with both arms the old paper factory's cold
spinning wheel

Thank you for telling me of this,

Using oyster shells as candle holders
I leaned against the wooden totem that tells people

about whales and seals

    Picturing the migration routes of the whales

    All the while, I waited for the deer to appear

      Just worry about yourself

      Do not care about other people

    The evenly outstretched antlers

    The dark eyes, staring at me, as I go to scoop water

from the well

    The huge body, like a horse

    with no disappearing scene

    I spoke no word until the candle burned all the way

down

    On this island

    Everyone said, they had never seen me

Rental

I am staying at a stranger's house

I walk out to the balcony

and watch the fountain in the garden across the street

It seems like the stranger is a woman

There are many types of body wash in the bathroom

As I crawled into bed

I paused when lifting the blanket

Is it all right?

In a dream where lions, grapes, and children appeared

I drank water,

contemplated seriously,

and fell from a great height

I watch the fountain from the balcony

There is a scent of roses

I lean my back against the warm heated steel of the chair

Earthquake

I went to the bathroom in the middle of interviewing
Hospice members at an office near Keio University
    While I was soaping my hands there was a fairly big
earthquake
    The grey walls shivered
    When I returned to the office
    All four elderly people waiting for the interview
    said they were worried I would be too shocked
    and were relieved to see how calm I was
    Their faces were all smiling as they looked at me
    But they were sitting with both arms hanging limply

Part 2

Brush

When I opened my eyes

My sister and brother were looking down at me

Wake up

They said

Uncle is dead

Because I did not know what 'dead' meant

I went to the sofa pushed into the corner

And asked, May I sleep more?

Like on a holiday, people came to my house

I was happy that my cousin came

Aunties kept crying

And cried again each time guests came

Look at Auntie, she tells people not to cry, but she can't stop crying

You're right. That's funny

After Gutpan* finished

My mom stroked my hair and said

Uncle might be a sparrow now

Because he was a really good person

That's when the tears came

When I opened my eyes

The neon blue of the video player

was blinking the wrong time as usual

* A kind of Korean funeral ceremony

First Drawing
– Oksoonbongdo*

The boatman stirs the paddle

Ferrying two men wearing Gats**

The slow, sly tone

of the one pointing afar

can almost be heard

The river Mom swam in as a child

The bridge my uncle tripped on

Might it be somewhere here?

I felt car sick on the river shores of Sangsunam

My father parked the car and smoked a cigarette near

Jungsunam

The strong current sprouts beneath my feet

And crashes into the boulder

One more step and I could die
sucked into it
But still I edge towards
the blue current

In the art museum, I press my face right up to the showcase,
And look at the men wearing Gats

It's called Oksoonbong
For its likeness to bamboo sprouts after the rain

* The first drawing in DanwonHwachep by Hong–Do Kim
** Korean traditional hats

The Last Sentence

Mom gave me her poem to read

I told her it was all good except the last sentence
which seemed a bit off
Mom got upset and said, What do you know, in
my whole life, I have read so many poems from the
newspaper
Now I see that you, who is majoring in literature,
know nothing about poems

That's not what I meant, I liked the first four verses
I like this because of that and that because of this
I even felt as if I had actually been to Mt. Geumgang
How did you come up with such a good expression,
after carefully telling her how I felt, I told her it was a
shame the last line felt like a diary

Mom got upset and said, What do you know about poems, I have read so many poems from newspapers, I win a prize in the writing contests every spring and fall

And my friend was amazed at how well it was written, so what's wrong with you

I was surprised to find out my mother was the kind of person who gets angry so easily

I did not say it was a bad poem

Can I not have my own opinion on one or two sentences

Did my honest criticism really hurt so much?

I thought to myself, my writer friends must have hearts of steel

At dinner I took a step back

Mom, I am not used to these expressions because I have not read enough poems

I told her carefully

But she replied, really you don't understand because you don't know

There is nothing wrong with the last sentence

I was surprised to find out my mother was the kind of person to stay angry for so long

For the first time ever it was not my mother, but Ms. Man-boon Heo I had made angry

Mom, I had another look at the poem and the last line is fine

I'm sorry about yesterday

I even apologized the next day

But she did not accept it

Mom is still writing poems

Even though she told me not to write about her

Somehow, I write about her often

Thinking back on it, Mom's last sentence was not that
much like a diary

Eyebrows, Shutter Speed Priority*

I don't know if there is a certain direction I should
kneel to
So I will face the window

With the light of the vending machine on my back
I pray

Please give us sleep
Please let sleep come
To my mother tonight

Please give to us, the sleep you give every night
Sleep to heal
Sleep to forget

The sleep you give generously every night to all

To the deer, the lion, and the doctor

When I meet the nurse outside the lounge

Her eyebrows slanted in pity come into focus

Everything else

becomes blurred

* Function for capturing moving objects

Fragrance of Fire

There was no one on the sand bank

I shivered for an hour at the bus stop

Waiting for the village bus

An empty Makgeolli* bottle

Where there was an old camp fire

Picturing someone I know

Sitting dazed

As if I saw a face, devoid of expression

Wavering in the heat

Across from the fire

The skin around my eyes stings

* Korean rice wine

Restaurant for One

The woman is having a Japanese home cooked meal
I can hear her eating

Is that woman a kind person?
What happened to her this late at night?

The woman is awkward at expressing herself
She recently overcame hard times

No, the woman is nothing like that
I don't know anything about her

Like a lion
I am adapting to all the ways
I react to the vegetation, elephants, and the humidity
Pinching my earlobe

124

Erase!

Today's ration of warmth is served in a bowl

The person next to me

eats it quickly and leaves

There is a purple flower drawn on the soup bowl

I don't know the name of it

I won't look it up

The next customer that comes in

adds to the list of people

I treat for who they are

To Mecenatpolis

I was seated in

a late night diner

Behind the man who was choosing his words
carefully

A bug was crawling up the wall

Behind you,

I said

And both of us looked at the bug climbing the wall

To the man with the reddened face who carefully
chose his words

I don't remember what I said no matter how hard I try

After some hesitation,

All I can remember is saying, behind you

Feeling too awkward to catch the bug

We both sat there looking at it

The house I lived in ten years ago

turned into a clothing shop and a real estate agency

The photo studio in front of Hapjeong Station exit no.5

shows the same family photo

Servomechanism

I teach classes at a small academy

When it is break time, I eat some kimbab and instant

cup noodles

Uttering words I don't know

I press the soft bark

of the Metasequoia that stands along the side of the road

Ship's steering gear: A 'Servomechanism' that keeps a

specific ship's course, instead of a human pilot

Servo mechanism: A controlling device that corrects the

random inputs to reach the set output of a mechanism

Ship's steering gear:

My shoes' memory power to take me back home

Servomechanism:

The entertainment show around 11 pm with Jae-suk Yoo

I recall all the large and small actions I took

In an unexpected order

With opposite temperature

Uttering words I don't know

I press the soft bark

of the Metasequoia that stands along the side of the road

Regretting enjoyments

Rejoicing in regrets

A Person I Know

A person I know, wanted a child after she got divorced, I thought of her as I was riding my bike A person I know, put five thousand won in my hand saying take a taxi, I thought of her as I was riding my bike A person I know, could not get an insurance, he cried and wiped his nose saying that the Mul-naengmyeon* was spicy, I thought of him as I was riding my bike

A person I know, could not get a job and went back to his country, his wife and son stayed here, I thought of him as I was riding my bike A person I know, erased me from her contacts, I thought of her as I was riding my bike

A person I know, crossed the street at a questionable moment, I thought of him as I was riding my bike

A person I know, learned Hangeul** without her daughter–in–law knowing, I thought of her as I was riding my bike A person I know bought a herb plant for a dry room but replaced it with a cactus later, I thought of her as I was riding my bike

A friend of a friend of a friend of a person I know, told me to invest in her business, I thought of her as I was riding my bike

A person I know, erased me from her contacts, I thought of a person I do not know as I was riding my bike A person I do not know, got Magnolias and Camelias mixed up, I thought of Magnolias and Camelias

* Cold buckwheat noodles
** The Korean alphabet

Mango

The academy decided to close down next month

I will be sad not to see my fifth grade student
Seungwon anymore

The American Independence Revolution that
Seungwon studies was from 1775 to 1783

I was surprised to realize that the Franklin who sits
next to Thomas Jefferson is the same Franklin who
made the lightening rod

Seungwon picks at his hair

I saw some blood on the crown of his head last fall

but now there is a bare patch the size of a coin

It is May

All school trips have been cancelled so children come
to the academy instead

We were supposed to arrive at Jeju Airport now

No, silly, we should have arrived earlier and gone to Ilchulbong by now

They raise their voices arguing about this, and spend five minutes asking for a five-minute break

Even with permission given they do not play

Instead they keep talking to me, telling me they have memorized the number of dead, missing and rescued

One says that in his dream he saw a wave as tall as a three-story-building

The other says, he dreamed he got trapped in the bathroom

This year I can see a lot of mangoes on the street

I didn't buy them before because they were too small, but the ones on this truck are quite big

They will grow bigger and contain fresh summer
inside their soft skin if I wait a little longer
   If we wait a little bit longer

   Was I thinking of mangoes···
   I cannot eat mangoes because my heart hurts

Close Relationship

I call her

She says she's on her way to buy milk

She doesn't speak about the gossip

When did her life get so complicated

Our time together does not explain anything about her

She never got a cold from breathing in the dawn air

She does not know the right riverside to crush empty

beer cans at

Or the bench of an old brick church that is good for

crying

Do I have to be born again?

But of course

When I asked her what she wanted to be in her next life

She rather answered me with a question

It is nice

to hear your voice

The sound of crushed fallen leaves

Right before the rain

is soothing

Unsure

I received a comic book as a gift

It was more a gift than a comic book

But it was so good

My sister's friend borrowed it

I told my sister it must be returned since it was a gift

But I did not get it back

My sister never told me who borrowed it

And only made awkward faces

I wanted to read the comic book again

So I borrowed it from my cousin who had a copy of it

   It's something I want to keep so please return it

She emphasized as she lent it

I loved reading it

Every time I met her I thought of returning it

But wanting to read it again I kept putting it off

But this is not a gift

It was not given to me as a gift

Early dawn, in a taxi

I reminisce about the comic book's whereabouts

Knowing why it is lost

Part 3

Retirement Celebration

Please come and join us
You are invited

The birthday
that I picked for myself

I have made up my mind to live differently

I will offer a drink to myself
and dance

Contracts, signatures, overtime pay, taxi fares, age,
mobile fees, growth rates, parents,
and people talk talk

Aah, too anxious

feeling so guilty

Let's throw a party
that changes all that to excitement
that turns it all into expectations

With your support
I look forward to it

No, just forget it all
and let's just meet up
retirement is just an excuse

At Noeul Park's camping site,
let's cook shrimp
with the people we cherish

Afternoon Cherry Blossoms

Cherry blossoms leap

Let's catch the wind that is coming in
I am going to ride that small whirlwind

Swirling
The wings of the butterfly that start the wind
And a petal which flies higher and higher

The fallen petal on the doorstep
How far has it traveled?

Soon it is time
for the visitor to arrive

Looking down at the cherry blossom tree
I listen to the waves of the trees

Railroad

The leaves of the Ghost weed

have a white background

and only a little green

The leaves are like flowers and the flowers are like

leaves

The railroad where trains no longer come and go

The café owner

came out to the street market

to browse used goods

The leaves are like flowers

and the flowers are like leaves

The leaves are like flowers,

but the flowers are like flowers?

Girls wearing school uniform pants walk on the
railroad
The old man who was yelling, now walks his dog
And a used good finds a new owner

Pure white asphalt
A meandering crosswalk
I now feel as fine as this afternoon
As I ponder all these things

The leaves of the Ginkgo tree
are turning into skyblue

Festival

We drank alcohol and held hands

And confessed our saddest stories

The wrong choices his older brother made in life

The story of her leaving him for all the wrong reasons

Jealousy, unfairness

Poverty not possible to solve

Crying as we listen to the stories of those whose hands

we hold

Someone ran back from the bathroom

And showed us a pill regurgitated

Saying, "It must have been stuck in my chest for 15 days."

We all stood up in joy

And about to clap and dance around the table

When from the window, a voice sounding surprisingly close despite the wall said,

"Please, let us sleep now,"

⋯The words of a neighbor

When I woke up

I could not see the pill we pulled out

Nodding off

I ran my fingers over a spot

Where I thought the pill might be

The One and Only

In this Matcha cake
There is wild strawberry jam

If it were up to me
I would have used Matcha only

Sister, without the taste of wild strawberry jam
It would be bland

Is that so?
Maybe that is why I am not good enough

Not good enough at what?

Huh?
(To be the one and only best writer)

A little more

I want to try just a little more and become

the one and only best writer

I need that wild strawberry jam!

Wild strawberry jam it is···

The taste of Matcha I was enjoying while holding

the tea bowl

And the green condensation

I exhaled

For me,

With only Matcha, please

What about becoming the one and only?

I just can't

Certain Ways to Look at Lights

I imagine the dreams you dream

In a very dark night

Holding a pink cigarette to your mouth

The taste of the cigarette is

Summer

To be honest

Nothing much happens in my dreams

I go here and there

I cry when I think it is not fair

I do not know why but

These places are so detailed

I imagine the dreams you dream

Like a child who tries to take the crayons

So she can draw it herself

No, more like

The feeling when she asks someone to draw a bird

In her sketchbook

The dream where you need to say you do not love someone

To show them you do

And where you need to say you love someone

To show them you do not

(To whom are you supposed to prove it to?)

With its back to the wall

A feeling that hides

Afraid to be caught by me

I dream a dream

Of someone who seems to be good at dreaming

The white bear on the alcohol bottle
The technique to wrap red bean buns quickly
The unknown word that calms me down
The poem that was released yesterday

Then can you dream
the dream you want?
Can you make
anyone show up in your dream?

If you really think about it a lot (laugh)
If you keep thinking about it before you fall asleep
(laugh)

For someone so unable to

I am captivated by a dream I had two days ago

I see a building on a hill from which you can look far out

It has a small restaurant on the first floor

I am with people close to me

But feel restless

Because I made someone wait

I can never be sure

But I am almost certain

that I must appear in other people's dreams

Nobody can choose the characters

If anyone appears

No one can cast them out

I can never be sure

But I am almost certain

I must have made you wait

I must have asked something of you

In that dream

The unknown word that calms me down

The poem that was released yesterday

I

Do not want to see the lights

In a certain way

'To stay in one's mind'

'To slip one's mind'

A refraction of a request

I dream a dream

Of someone who seems to be good at dreaming

As if my feeling comes close

And sits next to me

Mak*

I am focusing on two o'clock

Two o'clock is a sunny side up egg with a flat yolk

You are not like that, not as much as you think

My fallen heart when your face stiffened

I am focusing on two o'clock

Two o'clock is the problem of a dog that overslept, woke up, and still has nothing to do

The soccer game that I cannot remember

The words that I cannot remember saying

My heels while I was standing listening to you

I am focusing on three nineteen

It is like when the lengths and widths change as you lie down

It is like when the lengths and widths do not change although you do lie down

Smoothing the wrinkles of the white wrapping cloth

I was me

Even before you called my name

The flowers are still flowers even after you stepped
on them

I am focusing on three nineteen where the flowers
are cascading

The engine sound as it heads to the runway

The coincidence that determined the town I live in

The coincidence before that coincidence

The three nineteen of the night is crumpled

The three nineteen of the dawn is wavering and
scattered

The facial expression of the man who eats my

leftover noodles

    The clothes he wore that day

    Like drawing a bow and releasing,

    Four o'clock shoots and hits me

    Four o'clock is focusing on me

    The sadness of cutting a relationship

    The sadness of keeping a relationship

    The dreariness of longing for a time in my life when
I still felt longing

    The rear centered silhouette of an elephant–like
animal

    Four o'clock also leaves me behind

*The word '막' has many homonyms. Just, curtain, layer, membrane, wildly, stage, house, without hesitation.

Mint

My heart got larger

It is like a rock is grafted onto it

It is like running shoes are grafted onto it

It is like a rabbit is grafted onto it

Though I placed a flower petal on it

Though I hung it by the west window

I wonder why

It does not get smaller

In the bush where the cat hides

I make a doorframe

I pour olive oil

At the sound of the people doing the recycling

I cross out the stars with a red pen

Thud, thud, thud

I run as my feet plow holes into the track

A day being played at 1.25× the speed

Then why

I closed the curtains

I checked the front door

And I laid my heart on its side

It is fine if it is not

And that is actually a good thing

It is not important

And that is a good thing

My heart takes me along

Thud, thud, thud

It makes it hard to stand the heat

It makes two lives coincide

Ode to the Videotapes

There were such things called videotapes
They were the most romantic form of plastic

When someone said, "Do you want to go rent a
video?"
It had a different feeling than, "Wanna go watch a
movie?"

Because we made plans to watch videos
We gathered in Na–young's living room after the
exams finished
And have even been in the master bedroom of Su–
jung's house, whose mom was living in Seoul

The smell of film at the video store
was the smell of dust in the West where horses ran,

The smell of the water drop that Brigitte Lin threw
with her fingertips

The smell of a medieval knight's scabbard

The clarity of the 'click' when pressing the record
button

The relief when the shop owner discounted the late fee

The feeling of wanting to be extra nice from now on

The conclusion is this*

As video stores disappeared one by one

So were we separated

The faces of those times, when there was a video
store at every corner

are recorded here, close to my heart

* A play on the last stanza of Pablo Neruda's 「Ode to My Socks」.

에필로그

시를 쓰는 무수한 기쁨만큼
시집을 만드는 과정에 무수한 기쁨이 있다는 것을 알게
해 주신 이상영 사장님. 감사해요.

이수경 번역가님, 처음으로 번역된 저의 시를 받아 보았
던 순간은 잊지 못할 거예요. 감사합니다.

그리고 이 시집은
저를 가장 잘 아는. 가장 사랑하는 케빈이 감수해 주었
습니다.
조금이라도 케빈의 마음을 상하게 하는 시는 버리겠다
고 했는데
모든 시를 담을 수 있어 다행입니다.

항상 응원해 주신 분들 직접 뵙고 인사드릴 수 있다면
기쁠 것입니다.

읽어 주셔서 감사해요.

Epilogue

I want to thank Sang-young Lee who let me know there are as many countless delights in making a book as there are in writing poems.

The translator Su-Gyung Lee, I will never forget the moment I received my poems translated for the first time. Thank you.

The translation of this book of poetry was polished by Kevin who knows and loves me the most.
I told him I would delete any poem if it hurt him.
I am glad all my poems are in this book.

I hope I can see all the people who support me in person and thank them.

Thank you for reading.

김은지

시 쓰고 소설 쓰고 팟캐스트 만들고 그림 그려요. 시 모임 낭독회 기획하고 책방에서 책 주인을 찾아 주고 있습니다.

2016 《실천문학》 신인상 시 부문 당선
2017 아르코 유망작가 지원금 수혜
2017 독립출판 소설 『영원한 스타-괴테 72세』
2018 〈쓺〉에 단편소설 「산호섬」 발표
2019 『팟캐스터』 공저

팟캐스트 방송 〈세상엔 좋은 책이 너무나 많다 그래서 힘들다
(세너힘)〉 진행
책방에서 시 모임 진행
(지구불시착, 도도봉봉, 아무책방, 핏어팻)

강혜빈, 임지은, 한연희 시인과 '분리수거' 낭독회 개최
육호수 시인과 '여행에서 주운 시' 낭독회 개최

@ipparangee

Eun-ji Kim

I write poems and fiction. I make a podcast show and draw pictures.
I lead writing classes and plan recitals. At the bookstore I try to find the
right owners for the right books.

2016 won the 《Silcheonmunhak》 New Writer Award for poetry
2017 received the Arko Promising Writer Grant
2017 made the independent short story book 『Eternal Star—Goethe
　　　72 years old』
2018 released the short story 「Coral Island」 on 〈Sseum〉
2019 co-wrote the book 『Podcaster』

Currently making the podcast show 〈There are too many good books
in the world so it is hard〉
Hosting writing classes at independent bookstores
(Jigubulsichak, Dodobongbong, Anybookstore, Pit a pat)

Holding the recital 'Separate Collections' with Hye-bin Kang,
Ji-eun Lim, Yeon-hui Han
Holding the recital 'Poems we picked up on trips' with Ho-soo Yook

@ipparangee

이수경

이화여대 졸업 후 미국에서 석사. ㈜바른번역 한영번역가로 활동.
『책방에서 빗소리를 들었다』를 번역하면서 시를 다시 사랑하게
되었다.

Su-Gyung Lee

Graduated from Ewha University and received her Master's degree in the U.S. Translator associated with Barun Translators.
She revived her love for poetry after translating 『I Heard the Sound of Raindrops at the Bookstore』.

책방에서 빗소리를 들었다

2019년 3월 25일 1판 1쇄 발행
2022년 6월 1일 1판 2쇄 발행

지 은 이 김은지
번   역 이수경
발 행 인 이상영
편 집 장 서상민
디 자 인 서상민, 오진희
영문 감수 케빈 쿠스망
마 케 팅 정혜리
펴 낸 곳 디자인이음
등 록 일 2009년 2월 4일:제300-2009-10호
주   소 서울시 종로구 자하문로 24길 24
전   화 02-723-2556
메   일 designeum@naver.com
blog.naver.com/designeum
instagram.com/design_eum